EXPLORE OUTER SPACE

THE SUN

by Ruth Owen

WINDMILL
BOOKS.
New York

Published in 2014 by Windmill Books, An Imprint of Rosen Publishing
29 East 21st Street, New York, NY 10010

Produced for Windmill by Ruby Tuesday Books Ltd
Editor for Ruby Tuesday Books Ltd: Mark J. Sachner
US Editor: Sara Howell
Designer: Emma Randall
Consultant: Kevin Yates, Fellow of the Royal Astronomical Society

Photo Credits:
Cover, 4–5, 10, 22–23, 24–25, 26 © Shutterstock; 6–7, 29 © NASA, ESA, and the Hubble Heritage Team; 7 (top), 20–21 © Public domain; 8–9 © European Southern Observatory (ESO); 9 (top), 11 (top) © NASA/JPL-Caltech/R. Hurt (SSC); 11 (bottom), 15, 19 © NASA; 12–13 © EIT, SOHO Consortium, ESA, NASA; 16–17 © Science Photo Library; 23 (bottom) © Shutterstock/Ruby Tuesday Books Ltd.; 27 © NASA/ESA; 28–29 © NASA/JPL-Caltech/S. Stolovy (SSC/Caltech).

Library of Congress Cataloging-in-Publication Data

Owen, Ruth, 1967–
The sun / by Ruth Owen.
    p. cm. — (Explore outer space)
Includes index.
ISBN 978-1-61533-720-0 (library binding) — ISBN 978-1-61533-757-6 (pbk.) — ISBN 978-1-61533-758-3 (6-pack)
1. Sun—Juvenile literature. I. Title. II. Series: Owen, Ruth, 1967– Explore outer space.
QB521.5.O93 2014
523.7—dc23

                                            2012050219

Manufactured in the United States of America

CPSIA Compliance Information: Batch #BS13WM: For Further Information contact Windmill Books, New York, New York at 1-866-478-0556

CONTENTS

Twinkle, Twinkle, Little Star

On a cloudless night it's awe-inspiring to look up into the blackness of space and see thousands of bright, twinkling **stars**. It's easy to forget that there is one very special star that we see and even feel every day of our lives. That star is the Sun.

About 93 million miles (150 million km) from Earth, this huge ball of burning gases creates a brilliant light in the blackness of space, and forms the center of our **solar system**. It's impossible to tell from Earth, but the Sun measures about 870,000 miles (1.4 million km) across. That's as wide as 109 Earths set side by side.

It's easy to take the Sun for granted. It's always there, rising in the morning and setting in the evening. If there was no Sun, however, Earth would be a dark, frozen lump of rock. Without our own diamond twinkling up above the world so high, there would be no life on Earth!

That's Out of This World!

Light travels at about 186,500 miles per second (300,000 km/s). It takes light about eight minutes to travel from the Sun to Earth. So we always see what happened on the Sun eight minutes ago!

A heron prepares to settle for the night as the Sun sets.

The Sun rises, bathing a field of wheat in early morning sunshine.

What Is A Star?

For most of its life, every star in the universe is a massive ball of incredibly hot burning gas.

All stars live out their lives in the same pattern. They are born. Then they enter the main part of their life when they burn gas for millions or billions of years. Then, as their supply of gas runs out, they die.

During the main part of their life, stars are made up of approximately 71 percent hydrogen gas, 27 percent helium gas, and about two percent of other elements. They are powered by a process called nuclear fusion. Inside the core, or center, of a star, hydrogen atoms are fused together, creating larger helium atoms. As nuclear fusion takes place, it creates huge quantities of energy that is given off as light, heat, and radiation.

There are different types of stars. Red stars are the coolest stars, with surface temperatures of about 4,500 °F (2,500 °C). Yellow stars, like the Sun, have a surface temperature of around 9,900 °F (5,500 °C). Sizzling blue-white stars reach temperatures of about 72,000 °F (40,000 °C).

Stars in the Large Magellanic Cloud, which is one of the Milky Way's neighboring galaxies.

The Sun

Red supergiant
Antares

This image shows a size comparison between Antares and the Sun.

That's Out of This World!

Stars come in different sizes. The Sun looks enormous in the sky, but that's just because it's our nearest star. In comparison to other stars, the Sun is really just an average, or medium-sized, star. And compared to red supergiant stars, such as Antares, a red supergiant in our galaxy, the Milky Way, the Sun is tiny!

The Sun Is Born

About five billion years ago, the chemical ingredients for the Sun and everything in the solar system—including you—were floating in a beautiful cloud of gas and dust called a **nebula**.

Then, part of the cloud began to collapse on itself. Gas and dust collected, creating a massive sphere, or ball. As the sphere rotated in space, a disk formed around the sphere from the remaining gas and dust. Pressure built up as the material in the sphere was pressed together by **gravity**, causing the sphere's core to heat up and reach temperatures of around 18 million °F (10 million °C). Finally, the sphere ignited, and the Sun was born!

Inside the spinning disk, leftover matter from the formation of the Sun clumped together. This matter formed Earth, the other **planets**, their **moons**, and other objects in our solar system.

The Carina Nebula is a star factory in our galaxy, the Milky Way. It contains over 14,000 stars.

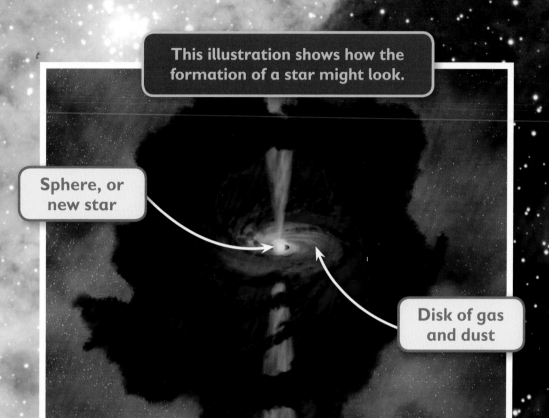

This illustration shows how the formation of a star might look.

Sphere, or new star

Disk of gas and dust

That's Out of This World!

Nebulae are clouds of gas and dust trillions of miles (km) wide. The word "nebula" is the Latin word for "cloud." Nebulae form in many different shapes and colors. They are the places where stars begin their lives and are often called "star factories" or "star nurseries."

THE SOLAR SYSTEM

Our solar system is made up of the Sun, eight planets, including Earth, and **dwarf planets**, such as Pluto and Sedna. The solar system also includes the planets' moons and objects such as **asteroids** and **comets**.

If you added up the **mass** of all the planets, dwarf planets, moons, and other objects in the solar system, their total mass would only add up to 0.5 percent of the entire mass of the solar system. The mass of the Sun accounts for the other 99.5 percent!

The Sun is so massive that its gravity pulls everything in the solar system toward it. That's why every object in the solar system continually orbits, or moves around, the Sun. Nothing can escape the gravitational pull of our huge star.

The solar system is also in orbit around the center of the Milky Way galaxy. Even though the solar system is moving through space at 157 miles per second (252 km/s), it takes between 225 and 250 million years to complete one orbit.

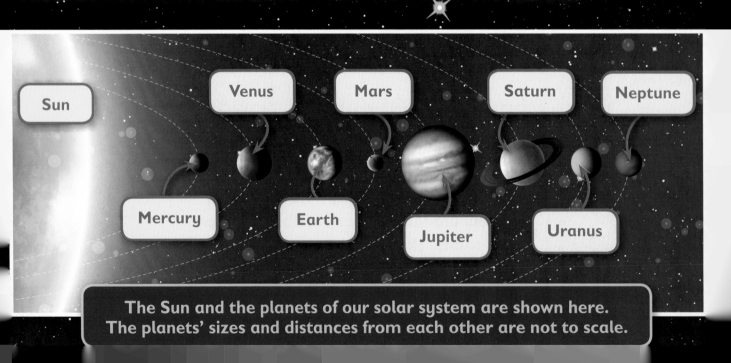

Sun · Venus · Mars · Saturn · Neptune · Mercury · Earth · Jupiter · Uranus

The Sun and the planets of our solar system are shown here. The planets' sizes and distances from each other are not to scale.

The orbit of the dwarf planet Sedna takes it to the farthest edges of the solar system. It takes the Earth 365 days, or one Earth year, to make a single orbit of the Sun. Sedna takes about 12,600 Earth years to complete one orbit! From the surface of Sedna, the Sun looks like a tiny, distant twinkle.

This illustration shows how the Sun probably looks from Sedna.

The Sun

Sedna

This artwork shows the Milky Way as if seen from above.

This dotted red line shows our solar system's orbit around the center of the Milky Way.

A Closer Look at the Sun

Like all stars, the **Sun** is made up of hydrogen and helium. It also contains a small quantity of other elements, including oxygen, carbon, and nitrogen.

The gases and other materials that make up the Sun form a kind of matter called **plasma**. Plasma is superheated matter that has become so hot that its atoms have lost some or all of their **electrons**.

Inside the huge, boiling mass of plasma that is the Sun, over 660 million tons (600 million t) of hydrogen are fused together every second to form 657 million tons (596 million t) of helium. The missing tons (t) are converted into energy.

It's impossible to imagine that quantity of energy, but here's one way to look at it. Take the amount of energy used in the United States in one year, multiply it by one million, and that's how much energy the Sun produces every second!

That's Out of This World!

The Sun is constantly rotating on its **axis**, just as the Earth does. Unlike a solid rocky planet, however, the Sun's plasma rotates at different speeds. At its north and south poles, the Sun rotates about once every 34 days. At its **equator**, the plasma rotates much faster, completing a rotation in about 25 days.

The sizes of the Sun, Earth, and Moon are not shown to scale.

The Moon
Radius = 1,080 miles
(1,738 km)

Earth
Radius = 3,959 miles
(6,371 km)

The Sun
Radius = 432,169 miles
(695,509 km)

INSIDE THE SUN

About 99 percent of the energy generated by the Sun through nuclear fusion is produced in its core.

In the Sun's core, temperatures reach 27 million °F (15 million °C). Here, the plasma is about 150 times denser than water.

Energy generated in the Sun's core is transported by photons. These high-energy particles travel out through the Sun's radiation zone and convection zone to the Sun's surface, or photosphere. From the photosphere, energy generated in the core streams into the Sun's **atmosphere** and out into space. It's this energy that lights and heats our planet.

The movement of photons from the Sun's core to its surface is not instant. In fact, it can take around 150,000 years for energy to reach the photosphere. This means the light from the Sun that you see today was produced when humans were still living in the Stone Age!

That's Out of This World!

The Sun's outer atmosphere is called the **corona**. Scientists do not know why, but while the temperature at the Sun's surface is 9,900 °F (5,500 °C), the corona's temperature is 1.8 million °F (1 million °C). That's like the air around a lightbulb being thousands of times hotter than the bulb's surface!

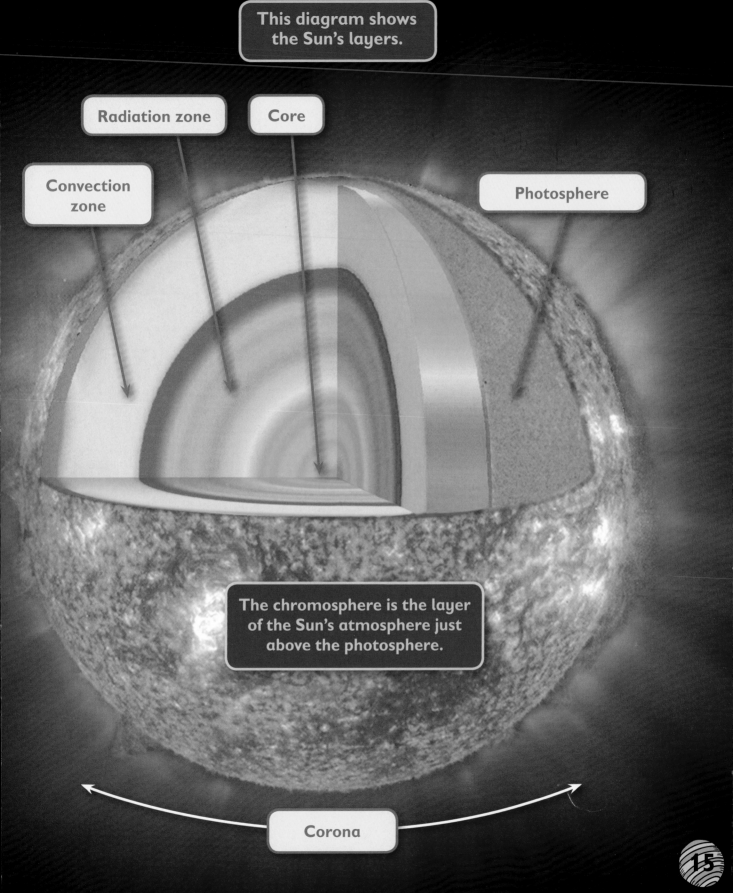

This diagram shows the Sun's layers.

Radiation zone

Core

Convection zone

Photosphere

The chromosphere is the layer of the Sun's atmosphere just above the photosphere.

Corona

SUNSPOTS

Among the phenomena that astronomers study on the Sun are sunspots.

Sunspots look like dark blotches on the Sun's bright surface. They are caused by magnetic activity blocking the flow of heat from inside the Sun to its surface. Sunspots look dark because they are cooler than the area around them.

Sunspots can be as large as 50,000 miles (80,000 km) in diameter. As they move over the Sun's surface, they expand and contract.

Scientists have discovered that activity on the Sun follows an 11-year cycle. During periods of high activity, hundreds of sunspots may be visible on the Sun in a day. Clouds of plasma and gas may also explode from the Sun's surface. These periods in time are known as the solar maximum. During years of low activity, known as the solar minimum, the Sun may go for days with little or no activity and no sunspots visible.

That's Out of This World!

Hundreds of years ago, astronomers wondered if sunspots might be cool areas on the Sun's surface where people could land. While cooler than surrounding areas, sunspots still reach temperatures of up to 8,000 °F (4,500 °C), so a spacecraft landing on a sunspot would be instantly melted!

The large sunspot group in this image from March 2001 had an area over 13 times bigger than the surface area of Earth!

SOLAR FLARES AND PROMINENCES

In addition to sunspots, beautiful phenomena called solar flares and solar prominences also occur on the Sun. A person should never look directly at the Sun because it will seriously damage their eyes. Astronomers only view the Sun through special telescopes that allow them to view the Sun safely on a computer screen.

A solar flare is a large burst of radiation from the Sun's surface. Solar flares may last for hours or for just a few minutes. These intensely bright phenomena look like explosions on the Sun.

A solar prominence is a massive, glowing loop of plasma that bursts out into the corona. Prominences are anchored, or connected, to the Sun in the photosphere. A prominence usually appears in just a single day, but it may last for several months.

That's Out of This World!

The glowing loop of a solar prominence may extend for hundreds of thousands of miles (km) out into space.

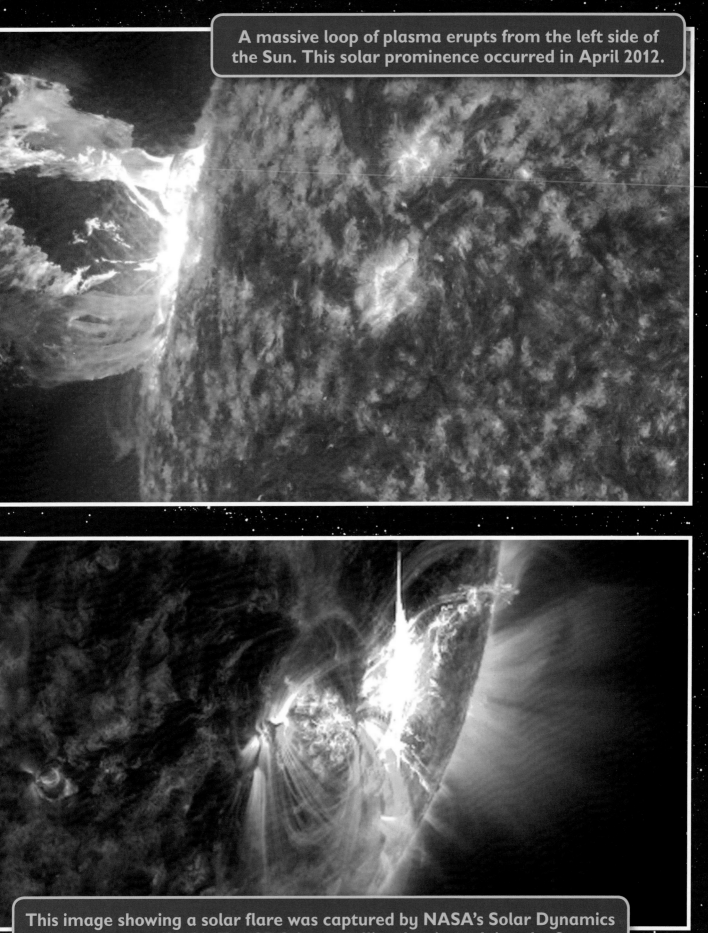

A massive loop of plasma erupts from the left side of the Sun. This solar prominence occurred in April 2012.

This image showing a solar flare was captured by NASA's Solar Dynamics Observatory (SDO). The SDO is a satellite that is studying the Sun.

19

THE SOLAR WIND

In addition to heat and light, the Sun also gives off a steady stream of particles known as the solar wind.

These particles are pieces of atoms that have become free from one another because of the intense heat of the Sun. The solar wind rushes out from the Sun in every direction at an average speed of 250 miles per second (400 km/s). Traveling this fast, the solar wind can complete the 93 million mile (150 million km) journey to Earth in just four days.

The solar wind spreads out from the Sun creating a kind of bubble that surrounds the solar system. This bubble is known as the heliosphere. When the solar wind reaches the outer edge of the solar system, it mixes with solar winds from other stars in the Milky Way.

Aurora may look like rays, streamers, or curtains of colorful light in the sky. Here, the aurora borealis lights up the night sky in Alaska.

That's Out of This World!

When atomic particles from the Sun enter Earth's atmosphere at the North and South Poles, they create beautiful, colorful light shows called "aurora" high in the sky. In the north, these lights are called the aurora borealis, or northern lights. In the south, they are called the southern lights, or aurora australis.

SOLAR ECLIPSES

Perhaps the most fascinating solar phenomena are **solar eclipses**. During a partial eclipse, a section of the Sun is covered by the Moon. During a total eclipse, however, the entire Sun disappears and day turns to night. So what causes these incredible events to happen?

For billions of years, the Moon has been orbiting Earth, and together, the Moon and Earth have been orbiting the Sun. This relationship between Earth, the Moon, and the Sun makes it possible for eclipses to happen.

When the Moon passes between the Sun and Earth, it creates two shadows. These are known as a penumbral shadow and an umbral shadow. Most of the time, these shadows miss the Earth. Sometimes, however, the orbits of Earth and the Moon are in just the right position, and the Moon's penumbral shadow falls on Earth. Then a partial eclipse happens. From the part of the world where the penumbral shadow falls, it's possible to see the Moon's dark disk cover part of the Sun.

That's Out of This World!

Astronomers, scientists, space fans, and TV and film crews will travel across the world for the chance to see and record solar eclipses. When viewing solar eclipses, people must wear specially-designed eye protectors or use specially-adapted telescopes.

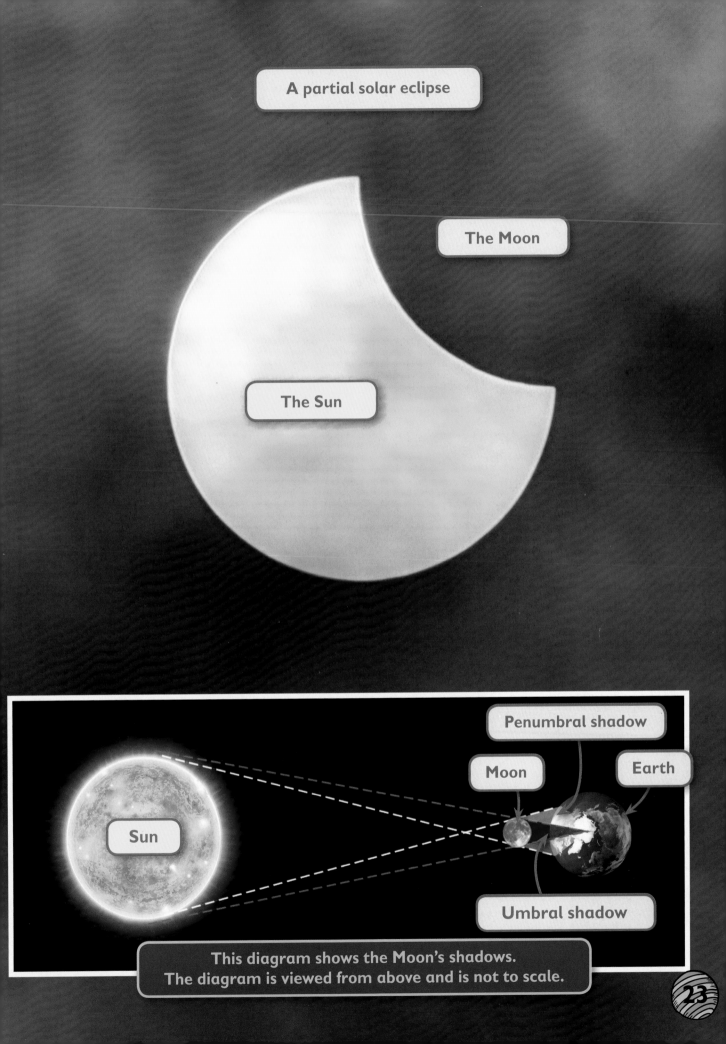

A partial solar eclipse

The Moon

The Sun

Penumbral shadow

Moon

Earth

Sun

Umbral shadow

This diagram shows the Moon's shadows.
The diagram is viewed from above and is not to scale.

23

TOTAL SOLAR ECLIPSE

Sometimes, when the orbits of the Moon, Earth, and Sun are just right, the Moon passes directly between the Earth and the Sun.

During a total eclipse, the Moon's umbral shadow falls on just a small section of Earth. From this area, it's possible to see the Moon completely block out the Sun, turning day to night for just a few minutes.

The math that makes total eclipses possible is amazing. The Moon is 400 times smaller than the Sun. The distance between Earth and the Sun, however, is 400 times greater than the distance between Earth and the Moon. This matching up of size and distance makes the Moon exactly the right size to completely eclipse the Sun.

A total eclipse happens somewhere on Earth about once every two years. As the Moon moves precisely into place to block out the Sun's light, stars appear, birds become quiet and stop flying, and animals get ready to go to sleep. The temperature may also drop by up to 60 °F (16 °C).

That's Out of This World!

The Sun's corona is not normally visible. As the Sun disappears behind the Moon during a total solar eclipse, however, the beautiful corona appears. Total eclipses give scientists an important opportunity to study this part of the Sun's atmosphere.

A total solar eclipse

The corona extends into space from the Sun's surface for millions of miles (km).

Starlight for Life

As a star, the Sun is not particularly special, and it has no unusual features. Like the estimated one to four billion or so other stars in the Milky Way, it is just a ball of burning gas. To every living thing on Earth, however, the Sun is essential.

One very important way that the Sun makes life on Earth possible is by providing us with food. Without starlight, we would have nothing to eat!

Plants survive by making their own "food." They take in water from the soil and carbon dioxide from the air. Then inside their leaves, they use sunlight to turn these ingredients into the energy they need to live and grow. This process is called photosynthesis. Without sunlight, plants could not exist, and without plants, humans and other animals would have nothing to eat. Even carnivorous animals need plants, because plant life feeds the prey animals that meat eaters feed on.

Sunlight makes life on Earth possible in another way, too. During photosynthesis, plants give off oxygen from their leaves. Without oxygen to breathe, no animals could survive on Earth.

Plants make oxygen.

Plants are food for humans and other animals.

An illustration showing SOHO in space

This image shows **SOHO** during its construction with engineers from the European Space Agency (ESA).

That's Out of This World!

Humans will never be able to visit the Sun, but from a distance, spacecraft have been studying it for decades. The Solar and Heliospheric Observatory (SOHO) was launched in December 1995. SOHO orbits the Sun, studying our star and sending data back to Earth.

THE DEATH OF THE SUN

Stars like our Sun may live for billions of years. Eventually, however, their supply of hydrogen fuel burns out. Then their lives come to an end. This will happen to our star in around 5 billion years.

As the Sun's fuel runs out, it will swell in size to become a red giant star. Its diameter will increase by up to 250 times. As it swells, it will swallow up Mercury and then Venus. Eventually Earth will come to a fiery end as it is engulfed by the Sun. After about a billion years, the Sun will begin to expel, or blow off, its outer layers. These layers of gas and dust will form a cloud, known as a **planetary nebula**. Finally, the remains of the Sun's core will collapse, leaving just a small, dense star called a white dwarf.

Where our Sun once burned, a beautiful nebula will be floating in the Milky Way. The Sun, our Earth, and everything on Earth, will have become a cloud of ingredients with the potential to one day become new stars and possibly new worlds.

This image shows hundreds of thousands of stars in the Milky Way galaxy.

White dwarf star

Cloud of gas and dust

This image shows a planetary nebula. Astronomers have named it the Necklace Nebula because of its shape.

That's Out of This World!

The remains of a star that have been squeezed by gravity to form a white dwarf are super compressed and dense. In fact, a piece of a white dwarf star the size of a sugar cube would weigh as much as two elephants!

GLOSSARY

asteroids (AS-teh-roydz) Rocky objects orbiting the Sun and ranging in size from a few feet (m) to hundreds of miles (km) in diameter.

astronomers (uh-STRAH-nuh-merz) Scientists who specialize in the study of outer space.

atmosphere (AT-muh-sfeer) The layer of gases surrounding a planet, moon, or star.

atoms (A-temz) The smallest particle of something, consisting of electrons, protons, and neutrons.

axis (AK-sus) A straight line about which a body, such as a planet, rotates.

comets (KAH-mitz) Objects orbiting the Sun consisting primarily of a center of ice and dust and, when near the Sun, tails of gas and dust particles pointing away from the Sun.

corona (kuh-ROH-nah) A layer of gases that forms the outer atmosphere of the Sun.

dwarf planets (DWAHRF PLA-nets) Objects in space that look and act like a planet but are much smaller.

electrons (ih-LEK-tronz) Particles in an atom that carry an electrical charge and makes electric current when they move.

elements (EH-luh-ments) Chemical substances that consist of only one type of atom and cannot be broken down into a simpler substance by a chemical reaction.

equator (ih-KWAY-tur) An imaginary line circling a body, such as a planet, which is an equal distance between its north and south poles.

galaxy (GA-lik-see) A group of stars, dust, gas, and other objects held together in outer space by gravity.

gravity (GRA-vuh-tee) The force that causes objects to be attracted toward other physical bodies.

mass (MAS) The total quantity of matter in a body.

Milky Way (MIL-kee WAY) The galaxy that includes Earth and the rest of our Sun's solar system.

moons (MOONZ) Natural objects that orbit a planet.

nebula (NEH-byuh-luh) Massive clouds of dust and gas in outer space. Many nebulas are formed by the collapse of stars, releasing matter that may, over millions or billions of years, clump together to form new stars.

nuclear fusion
(NOO-klee-ur FYOO-zhun) A nuclear reaction in which atoms fuse together to form larger atoms, releasing energy in the process.

phenomena (fih-NAH-muh-nuh) Unusual or exceptional events or things.

planets (PLA-netz) Objects in space that are of a certain size and that orbit, or circle, a star.

planetary nebula
(PLA-neh-teh-ree NEH-byuh-luh) A nebula formed from a dying star that has a rounded shape, like a planet.

plasma (PLAZ-muh) A superheated form of matter.

radiation (ray-dee-AY-shun) Energy that is radiated in waves or in particles.

red supergiant (RED SOO-per-jy-int) A star that is far larger than most others, which is nearing the end of its life cycle.

solar eclipses (SOH-ler ih-KLIPS-es) Events in which the Sun is fully or partially blocked from view by the Moon passing in front of it.

solar system (SOH-ler SIS-tem) The Sun and everything that orbits around it, including asteroids, meteoroids, comets, and the planets and their moons.

stars (STARZ) A body in space that produces its own heat and light through the release of nuclear energy created within its core.

universe (YOO-nih-vers) All of the matter and energy that exists as a whole, including gravity and all the planets, stars, galaxies, and contents of intergalactic space.

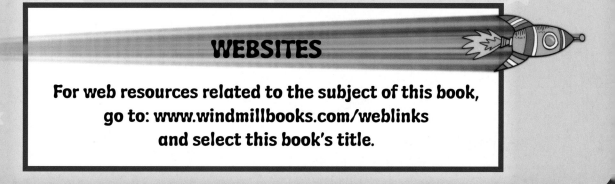

WEBSITES

For web resources related to the subject of this book, go to: www.windmillbooks.com/weblinks and select this book's title.

READ MORE

Croswell, Ken. *The Lives of Stars*. Honesdale, PA: Boyds Mill Press, 2010.

Landau, Elaine. *The Sun*. A True Book. Danbury, CT: Children's Press, 2008.

Simon, Seymour. *The Moon*. New York: Simon and Schuster Books for Young Readers, 2004.

INDEX